# THE BEST WEEK EVER

## By Eleanor Robins

T 31220

P

Development: Kent Publishing Services, Inc.
Design and Production: Signature Design Group, Inc.
Illustrations: Jan Naimo Jones

SADDLEBACK PUBLISHING, INC.
Three Watson
Irvine, CA 92618-2767

Website: www.sdlback.com

ISBN 1-56254-677-5

Printed in the United States of America

2 3 4 5 6   08 07

The Best Week Ever

Eleanor Robins
AR B.L.: 2.4
Points: 1.0

UG

# Chapter 1

Deb was at her locker. Val was at her locker too. Val was Deb's best friend.

Val said, "Steve will be out of town this weekend. Do you want to do something Saturday afternoon?"

Steve was Val's boyfriend.

"Sure. What?" Deb said.

Val said, "I don't know. We can think about it."

"OK," Deb said.

Deb saw Ben. He was in her math class. And he was Steve's best friend.

Ben was very cute. Deb wished he would ask her for a date.

"Does Ben have a girlfriend?" Deb asked.

Val said, "Not that I know of. He did. But they broke up. And she dates someone else now."

The girls hurried to their history class. It was their last class of the day. Miss Brent was their teacher.

The girls went to their desks. Val had to sit on the other side of the room. So she and Deb couldn't sit together.

The bell rang. Miss Brent started class. She always started class on time.

"Today we will talk about what you had to read for homework. And we won't read in the book," Miss Brent said.

Deb was glad they wouldn't read in the book. She didn't read well. So she could read only a little of the history book. Her mom had read the homework to her.

Miss Brent called on Deb first. And Deb was able to answer what Miss Brent asked her.

Miss Brent said, "Good answer, Deb."

That made Deb feel good.

Deb didn't have to try to read the book. So the class went by fast for her.

It was almost time for the class to be over.

Miss Brent said, "Don't forget you will have a test tomorrow. It will be a hard test. So you will need to study a lot for it."

Deb always studied a lot for the tests.

She could not read most of what was on the tests. But Miss Brent taped the tests for her. So she did not have to know how to read them. And Miss Brent gave her more time on the tests when she needed it.

Miss Brent let Deb write very short answers. And she did not count off for spelling.

But Deb still did not do well on the tests. It was hard for her to remember what she had studied.

It was going to be a bad week for her. It always was when she had a history test.

# Chapter 2

The bell rang.

Deb got up to go. But Val wasn't ready to go. She was talking to Tess. Tess sat next to Val.

They talked for a few minutes. Then Tess hurried out of the class.

Val came over to Deb.

Val said, "Tess is coming over to my house today. We are going to study for the test. Do you want to study with us?"

Deb said, "Thanks. But Mom doesn't want me to study with my friends."

Her mom thought the girls would talk too much. And not study. And her mom knew Deb had to study a lot.

"I know your mom wants you to study by yourself. But maybe it would help you to study with us," Val said.

Deb didn't say anything.

"Let's ask Miss Brent what she thinks," Val said.

"OK," Deb said.

The girls walked over to Miss Brent.

Val said, "Tess and I study for the tests together. And that helps us to do better. Do you think it would help Deb to study with us?"

"Why don't you wait in the hall, Val? And Deb and I will talk about it," Miss Brent said.

"OK," Val said.

Val hurried out in the hall.

Miss Brent said, "Do you want to study with Val and Tess?"

"Oh, yes. But my mom doesn't want

me to study with friends. She thinks we would talk too much. And not study," Deb said.

"Val and Tess have been doing well on their tests. So I think they study a lot. And not just talk," Miss Brent said.

"Do you think it would help me to study with them?" Deb asked.

Miss Brent said, "It might. Some people learn best with their eyes. Some learn best with their ears. Don't you learn best when you hear things?"

"Yes," Deb said.

"I think it would help you to talk about history with your friends. That might help you to remember it. You would be studying with your ears," Miss Brent said.

"Thanks, Miss Brent. I'll tell my mom that," Deb said.

Deb hurried out into the hall. Val

was waiting for her.

"What did Miss Brent say?" Val asked.

"Miss Brent thinks it is a good idea. But are you sure you want to study with me?" Deb said.

"Yes. Why did you ask?" Val said.

"Because I don't read well," Deb said.

Val said, "That doesn't matter. Tess and I will do all the reading."

"I'll ask my mom as soon as I get home," Deb said.

Deb asked her mom when she got home. And her mom said she could study with them just one time. And then see how she did on the test.

Val lived down the street from Deb. Deb hurried over to her house. She studied with Val and Tess for a long time.

Val and Tess did all of the reading. And Deb helped them to understand some of the things they read.

Deb thought she did well on her test the next day. So she thought it helped her to study with them. But she wouldn't know until she got her test back.

# Chapter 3

Deb was eating lunch with Val on Friday.

Val said, "We might get our history tests back today. The other classes got their tests back."

"I hope we did OK," Deb said. But she was sure Val did.

"I hope we did too. I got my math test back. So I need a good test grade today," Val said.

"What did you get?" Deb asked.

Deb didn't have to read a lot in math. So she always got good grades in math.

Val said, "I got a low C. There was only one good grade. That new boy Ed got an A. But he always does. Tess said he gets all A's in English and science too."

"I'm sure you got a good grade on the history test," Deb said.

"I think you did too," Val said.

Deb thought she did. But she wouldn't know until she got the test back. She could hardly wait to get to her history class.

Deb got to class early. Miss Brent started class as soon as the bell rang. Miss Brent said they were going to get their test papers back.

Val had been right. They were going to get their tests back.

Miss Brent said, "Griff, pass out these papers for me."

Griff started to pass out the papers. Deb wished Miss Brent would not let Griff pass them out. The test papers were folded. But he always looked inside to see the grades. And sometimes he would say something about them.

Griff passed out some of the papers.

He got to Deb's desk and stopped. He said, "Good for you. This is better than last time. Maybe I should study with you."

Was that his way of asking her for a date?

He handed Deb her paper. Deb quickly looked at her grade. She had gotten a B. It was a good week for her after all.

She could hardly wait to tell Val her grade. And to find out what Val got.

"She got a B too," Griff said.

"Who did?" Deb asked.

Griff said, "Val. I knew you wanted to know what she got."

Deb didn't like it when Griff looked at the grades. Why did he have to be in her class?

Deb wished Ben were in the class. And not Griff.

Deb could hardly wait for class to be over. She wanted to tell Val her grade. And she wanted to get home to tell her mom.

The bell rang.

Val hurried over to Deb's desk. She said, "What did you get, Deb?"

"I got a B," Deb said.

"Great, Deb. Tess and I did too," Val said.

Deb and Val quickly went to their lockers. And then they started to walk home.

For a few minutes they talked about their history tests.

Then Deb said, "I sure am glad it's Friday. And school is over for the week."

"Me too. No more classes for two days," Val said.

"Do you want to play some tennis tomorrow afternoon?" Deb asked.

"I can't. I have a date with Steve," Val said.

Deb was surprised. She thought Steve was going out of town. She had planned to go to the football game with Val. But now Val would want to go with Steve. So who would go with her? She didn't want to go by herself.

"I thought Steve had to go out of town," Deb said.

Val said, "He does. But not until his dad gets off work. So we have time to go to a movie. He didn't tell me until after lunch."

"Can you still go to the game with me?" Deb asked.

Val said, "Sure. What time do you want me to be at your house?"

"About 7:00. Is that time OK with you?" Deb said.

Val said, "Sure. I should be home by 5:30 or 6:00."

The girls didn't talk for a few minutes. Deb was thinking about Val's date with Steve. And Ben was Steve's best friend. So that made her think about Ben. She wished she could go to the show with him.

Then Deb said, "I wish Ben would ask me for a date. Then maybe the four of us could go some places together."

Val said, "That would be fun. Maybe Ben will ask you for a date."

They walked by Mrs. Clark's house. She lived next door to Deb. A lot of leaves were in her yard.

Val looked at the leaves. She said, "Mrs. Clark needs to rake her leaves."

Deb said, "She can't. She has been sick."

Val said, "I didn't know that. Too bad we can't rake them for her tomorrow. I sure am glad we raked our leaves last week."

"Me too," Deb said.

The girls had been busy the weekend before. Deb had helped Val rake her yard. Then Val had helped Deb.

The girls were in front of Deb's house.

Deb said, "Do you want to come in?"

Val said, "I can't. I need to get home. But I'll try to call you tonight."

Deb said, "Good. We need to talk about what to wear to the game."

Val hurried off.

Deb started to go in the house.

She looked over at Mrs. Clark's yard before she did. She hoped Mrs. Clark had someone to rake her leaves.

# Chapter 4

Deb went in the kitchen. Her mom was there. Her mom had been to the store. She was putting the food away.

Her mom said, "Hi, Deb. I thought I heard you come in."

Deb put her books on the table. Then she said, "I got my history test back, Mom. I got a B. I got a B."

Her mom said, "That is great news, Deb. Then it helped for you to study with Val and Tess."

"It sure did," Deb said.

"Maybe you can study with them next time," her mom said.

Deb hoped she could too.

"Do you have much homework?" her mom asked.

"No. Just a little," Deb said.

"Then maybe it won't take you long to do it," her mom said.

"It's math. So I don't think it will," Deb said.

"Do you have any plans this weekend?" her mom asked.

"Just to go to the game with Val. I asked her to play tennis tomorrow afternoon. But she has a date with Steve. It will be a long day with nothing to do," Deb said.

"You will find something to do," her mom said.

"Like what?" Deb asked.

Val had a date. So she would be too busy to do something with Deb.

"You could rake Mrs. Clark's leaves.

I went over to see her today. She's worried about how her yard looks. She thought her son was going to rake her leaves tomorrow. But he has to work."

"I would have to rake and bag them by myself. And that would be a lot of work," Deb said.

It had been OK to rake leaves with Val. But it wouldn't be any fun to do it by herself.

"I didn't say you had to do it. That was just a thought," her mom said.

But what else was there for Deb to do? She didn't want to sit around the house all day.

Deb said, "I'll call Mrs. Clark. And tell her I'll rake her leaves."

"Her number is by the phone," Deb's mom said.

Deb called Mrs. Clark. She told Mrs. Clark she would rake her leaves.

Mrs. Clark said, "That is very nice of you, Deb. Is someone going to help you?"

"No," Deb said.

"But that will be too much work for you," Mrs. Clark said.

"It won't be. It will be fun," Deb said.

But Deb knew it wouldn't be.

Val would be having fun. And she would be working hard.

Deb wished she had a date like Val did.

# Chapter 5

Deb helped her mom put the rest of the food up. And her mom started to make a cake.

Deb said, "I don't have much homework. So I think I will do it now."

She could do it all in an hour. Then she wouldn't have to think about it over the weekend.

Her mom said, "Do it here at the table. And I will do the reading for you."

Deb started to do her homework. She worked on it for about 15 minutes.

Then the phone rang.

Deb hurried to the phone. She hoped it was Val. And it was.

Val said, "Steve just called. I told him what you said."

"About what?" Deb asked.

Val said, "About wanting to date Ben. And about wanting the four of us to go places together."

"Oh, no. What did Steve say?" Deb asked.

Val said, "He liked the idea. And I have some good news for you."

"What?" Deb asked.

Val said, "He called Ben. And asked Ben to go to the movie with us. Ben said he would. Do you want to go too?"

"Yes. Yes," Deb almost yelled at Val.

Val laughed. She said, "Not so loud, Deb. I can hear you."

"Is Ben going to call me?" Deb asked.

Val said, "No. This isn't a real date. It is just sort of like a date."

"What do you mean?" Deb asked.

They were all four going to the movie. So how could it not be a date?

"Steve and I will come by and get you. And Ben will meet us at the movie," Val said.

So it wasn't a date. And Ben might not know Deb would be there too.

Deb said, "Then Ben doesn't know I'll be there."

Val said, "Yes, he does. Steve told him you were going with us. And that Steve wanted him to go too. Because you were going. Ben could have said no. But he didn't."

Val was right. He could have.

"Maybe Ben will ask you for a real date later," Val said.

"Maybe he will," Deb said. She sure hoped he would.

Val said, "Then it's all set. Now let's talk about what we should wear."

The girls talked about that for a while.

Then Val said, "I have to get off the phone. Mom wants me to do something. Steve and I will be by to get you about 2:00."

"OK," Deb said.

"See you then," Val said.

It would not be a real date. But it would almost be one.

Deb could hardly wait.

It wasn't just a good week for her. It was a great week.

# Chapter 6

Deb hurried to find her mom. She couldn't wait to tell her mom the news.

"Mom, I have great news," Deb said.

Her mom said, "It must be. What are you so happy about?"

Deb told her.

"Are you talking about tomorrow?" her mom asked.

"Yes," Deb said.

"Did you forget something?" her mom asked.

"What?" Deb asked. She couldn't think of anything she had forgot.

Her mom said, "Mrs. Clark's leaves. You told her you would rake them."

Deb said, "Oh, no. I forgot all about that."

How could she forget about that?

"What am I going to do? I can't do both," Deb said.

Her mom said, "You have to call Mrs. Clark. Or Val. And say you can't do what you said you would do."

How could Deb call Val? She wanted to go to the movie with Ben. That might get him to ask her for a date.

But how could she call Mrs. Clark? Mrs. Clark needed her leaves raked. And there was no one else to rake them.

Deb said, "I don't know what to do. I need some time to think about it."

Her mom said, "Don't take too long. Because they are both counting on you."

Deb thought for a few minutes about what she should do. But she knew. She didn't need to keep thinking about it. It was no longer a great week for her.

Slowly Deb went to the phone. She called Val.

Val said, "I'm glad you called. I was just about to call you."

"Why?" Deb asked.

Val said, "It's about Ben."

"What about him?" Deb asked.

Had he backed out of going?

Val said, "He might ask you to the game. It's OK to go with him. Don't worry about me. My dad can drive me to the game. And then come back and get me."

Val was a good friend. Not all friends would have said that.

"So why did you call?" Val asked.

Deb didn't want to tell Val. But she had to tell her.

"I can't go to the movie," Deb said.

"Why?" Val asked.

"I told Mrs. Clark I would rake her leaves. I forgot about that when you called," Deb said.

Val said, "Oh, no. I'm sorry, Deb. I know how much you wanted to go with Ben."

"Do you think Steve and Ben will get mad?" Deb asked.

Val said, "I don't know. I hope not. Maybe Steve will try to work this out again for you."

But Val didn't sound like she really thought he would.

# Chapter 7

The next morning Deb called Val. She wanted to find out what Steve said.

She said, "What did Steve say, Val? Was he mad?"

Val said, "No. I'm glad you called. I was getting ready to call you."

"Why?" Deb asked.

Val said, "To tell you what Steve said. I told him last night. He called me this morning. He said Ben is still meeting us at the movie."

"He is?" Deb said. She was surprised. Ben knew Steve and Val had a date.

Val didn't answer right away. Then she said, "I don't want to tell you this,

Deb. But Ben is bringing a date."

"I thought he and his girlfriend had broken up," Deb said.

Val said, "They have. He hasn't dated this girl before. This will be their first date. He called her last night after Steve said you couldn't go."

Why did Deb tell Mrs. Clark she would rake her leaves? She could be the one going to the movie with Ben. And not some other girl.

"Now I won't get to date Ben. They will like each other. And want to have more dates," Deb said.

Val said, "You don't know. They might not want to date each other again."

Deb didn't want to talk anymore. She said, "I'll let you go. I know you have a lot to do."

Val said, "I do. But I need to ask you

something. What are you wearing to the game tonight?"

The girls talked a few minutes about what to wear.

Then Val said, "See you about 7:00."

Deb's mom came in the room. She said, "I can see you are upset, Deb. What's wrong? Who was that on the phone?"

Deb said, "Val. Steve told Ben I couldn't go to the movie. And Ben asked another girl to go with him."

Her mom said, "I'm sorry, Deb. But he isn't the only boy."

That was easy for her mom to say. She wasn't the one who wanted to date Ben.

Deb said, "I'm going to start raking the leaves now. Then I will stop for a while. And rake the rest of them after lunch."

"That sounds like a good idea. Then you won't get as tired," her mom said.

Deb might not get as tired. But she still would not have any fun.

# Chapter 8

Deb got a rake from her garage. Then she went over to Mrs. Clark's house. She rang the front doorbell. Mrs. Clark opened the door.

Deb said, "Good morning, Mrs. Clark. I'm going to start raking your leaves now."

Mrs. Clark said, "Thank you, Deb. I have some leaf bags by the back door. But I think I need some more. I called the store. Someone there will bring me some more. The bags should be here in a little while."

Deb said, "I'll get the bags by the door. But it may be after lunch before I need them."

Deb walked out in the yard. She started to rake. It wasn't any fun to rake by herself. It had been fun when she and Val did it. They had talked all the time.

Deb started to get tired. She was ready to quit. But she would not quit.

A car stopped in front of Mrs. Clark's house. A boy got out.

He said, "This must be where Mrs. Clark lives. Am I right?"

"Yes," Deb said.

Deb had not seen him before. So she wondered who he was.

He opened the car door. He got out some leaf bags.

He said, "Is your mom home?"

Deb said, "Mrs. Clark is home. But she is not my mom. I live next door. I'm just over here to rake the leaves.

Mrs. Clark has been sick. And she can't rake them."

Mrs. Clark opened the front door. She came out in the yard. She had some money in her hand.

Mrs. Clark said, "I saw you drive up. I thought you must have my leaf bags."

Mrs. Clark paid the boy.

Then she said, "I haven't seen you at the store. How long have you been working there?"

The boy said, "I just moved here. My uncle owns the store. I help him some on the weekends."

Mrs. Clark said, "What is your name?"

"Ed," the boy said.

"Thank you for bringing my leaf bags, Ed," Mrs. Clark said.

Then she went back in the house.

Ed looked over at Deb. She was still raking the leaves.

"Is someone going to help you rake the leaves?" he asked.

Deb said, "No. But I sure wish I had some help."

"Are you going to do all the work this morning?" Ed asked.

"No. I'm going to stop in a little while. And do the rest of the work after lunch," Deb said.

Ed said, "I would be glad to help. But I have to get back to the store."

He got in the car and drove off.

He said he would be glad to help Deb. But Deb didn't think he really would like to help her.

# Chapter 9

Deb worked for about an hour longer. She didn't work very fast. Then she went home to rest for a while. And to eat lunch.

Her mom was cooking lunch. She said, "I saw you talking to that boy, Deb. I haven't seen him before. Who is he?"

"His name is Ed. He just moved here. Mrs. Clark needed some more leaf bags. And he brought them to her. He works at the store. His uncle owns the store," Deb said.

Her mom said, "Ed is cute. Does he have a girlfriend?"

"I don't know. I have never seen him before," Deb said.

Her mom was right. He was cute. Did he have a girlfriend? And would she ever see him again?

Deb and her mom ate lunch. Deb was in no hurry to go back to work. So she rested for about an hour after lunch. Then she went back to Mrs. Clark's yard.

Deb started to rake leaves. She wished she had someone to help her. It would be fun then. And the work would go faster.

Deb saw a car coming down the street. It looked like Ed's car. Could it be his car?

The car stopped. It was Ed's car. Ed got out of the car.

He said, "Need some help?"

"I sure do," Deb said.

Ed got a rake out of the back of his car.

"Thanks for coming back," Deb said.

Ed said, "I wanted to stay this morning. But I had to get back to work. I asked my uncle for the afternoon off. I told him you needed some help."

"Tell your uncle thanks too," Deb said.

Ed put his rake on the grass. He said, "Let's bag some leaves. You hold the bags. And I'll put the leaves in."

"OK," Deb said.

Deb held the bags. And Ed filled the bags with leaves. Then they started to rake the rest of the leaves.

Time was passing quickly. And Deb was having a good time. It wasn't hard work with someone to help.

"Where do you go to school?" Deb asked. She thought it must be Carter High. But she had never seen him there.

Ed said, "Carter High. I know you

go there. I've seen you there. I wondered what your name was. And I still don't know."

Deb said, "Sorry. I forgot you didn't know my name."

Deb told him her name.

Then Ed said, "I'm Ed Davis."

Ben's last name was Davis too. Was Ed his cousin?

"Is Ben Davis your cousin?" Deb asked.

Ed said, "No. But I know him. My first name is Ben too. We got the wrong class cards on the first day of school. I had to go to the office to get my card. And I sort of met him there. Is he your boyfriend?"

"No," Deb said.

But she had wanted him to be until she met Ed.

"We have a game tonight. Are you going?" Ed asked.

"Yes," Deb said.

"Who are you going with? Maybe I know him," Ed said.

Deb said, "I'm not going with a boy. I'm going with my best friend Val. Her boyfriend will be out of town. So we are going together."

"Do you want to go with me?" Ed asked.

Deb didn't know what to say. She had told Val she would go with her. And it was too late to back out on Val now.

Deb said, "I would like to go with you. But I told Val I would go with her. And it's too late to tell her I can't."

Ed said, "She could go with us. Unless you think her boyfriend wouldn't like it."

"I think it would be OK with him," Deb said.

Ed said, "I might know Val. A girl named Val is in my math class."

Oh, no. He must be that Ed. The one Val had told her about. The new boy Ed who got all A's.

"Are you the boy who gets all A's?" Deb asked.

"Almost always. Why?" Ed said.

"Val told me there was an Ed in her math class. And that he gets all A's," Deb said.

"Then I guess it is the same Val. What time should I be at your house?" Ed asked.

Ed got all A's. He wouldn't want to date a girl who didn't read well.

"I can't go out with you after all," Deb said.

Ed looked very surprised. He said, "Why? Because I get all A's?"

It was Deb's turn to be surprised. She said, "Why do you think that?"

"Some girls don't want to date a boy who gets all A's," Ed said.

"But that isn't why I can't date you," Deb said.

"Then why?" Ed asked.

Deb didn't want to tell him she didn't read well. But she had to tell him.

He would find out. And it was better for him to find out now. And not after they had a date. Because then he would say he didn't want to date her. And it would be better not to date him at all.

"I don't read well," Deb said.

Ed looked very surprised. He said, "What does that have to do with going to the game with me?"

"Some boys don't date a girl who can't read well," Deb said.

Ed said, "I don't know about that. But I do know this. I want to date you. Do you want to date me?"

"Yes," Deb said.

Ed said, "Good. What time should I be at your house?"

"Val should be there by 7:00. Is 7:10 OK with you?" Deb said.

"That's fine with me," Ed said.

Deb could hardly wait to tell Val about Ed.

Deb was glad she was raking Mrs. Clark's leaves. And not at the movie with Ben.

It wasn't a bad week for her after all. It was the best week ever. She had gotten a B on her history test. And she might have a new boyfriend.